For my own wonderful Amelia, with love.

First Published: April 2021 by Greatwood Books

Interior illustrations by Sam Meadows

www.rosewaterbrook.com

ISBN: 978-1-914297-00-7

LOST PUPPY
AT
CHRISTMAS

AMELiA'S ANiMALS BOOK 1

Contents

1

A Strange Sound

"Hurry up, Amelia, you don't want to be late for the last day of school!" Sally shouted up the stairs. Amelia threw on her cardigan and grabbed her bag from the floor of her room. She tried hard to be on time, she really did, but every day the morning just seemed to disappear.

"I'm coming, Mum," she called down, stopping just long enough to stuff her reading record into the front pocket of her bag. She thundered down the stairs, jumped the last two, and landed right in front of her mother. Sally smiled and held out Amelia's coat. It was the last day of school before the Christmas holidays, and the weather outside was cold and gloomy.

Amelia pulled her coat on and followed her mother out of the front door. They walked to school together every day. It was over a mile away, but Amelia didn't mind. She enjoyed the fresh air and being outside, and she always saw something interesting on the walk.

 8

"Look, can you see the dew on the grass this morning?" Amelia said. "It looks like someone scattered diamonds everywhere!" The morning sun glittered on the dewdrops, making them sparkle.

"It's lovely. Can you smell the air? I think it will be frosty tonight. Maybe those diamonds will turn into pearls," Sally said, smiling.

Amelia went to the only school in Little Ridlington, a small market town deep in the English countryside. She liked school, but she was really looking forward to the Christmas holidays. Sally worked in an accountant's office in the town square, close to the school. Amelia knew that her mother didn't really

9

enjoy work. Sally was good with numbers and got on well with people. However, her boss, Mr. Gunder, always seemed to be shouting about something. Amelia didn't like him at all. Her mother said that Mr. Gunder was permanently angry and not to take it personally.

Not far from their house, they walked past a broken gate in a hedgerow leading on to a ploughed field. Amelia thought she heard a rustling and a small crying sound on the other side of the hedge.

"Mum, what's that?" They both stopped to listen, but the sound didn't come again. "Can we go in the field and look?" Amelia asked.

 10

Sally looked concerned. "Yes, let's have a little look. It sounded like a hurt animal."

They jumped over the gate and started searching around the corner of the field. There were some animal footprints in the wet mud. Amelia followed them; they seemed to go into a dense hawthorn bush. She crouched down and tried to peer into the branches. It was dark, and full of old autumn leaves that had blown under the hedge. She couldn't see any animals.

Amelia stood up and looked around. They were standing in a bare, ploughed field with hedgerows. There were puddles in some of the furrows from all the rain they had been having

11

recently. A large overflow pipe emerged from the bank at the end of the field, next to the ditch. Sheep grazed in the next field over, and beyond that there was an enormous house with fancy shaped hedges she hadn't seen before.

"What's that place over there?" Amelia asked, pointing.

"Oh, that's the manor house. In the old days, it was where the local lord lived who owned all the farms and land nearby. Once, there would have been dances and fancy dinner parties there. There were big stables, and lots of people worked at the manor. These days, it's just Lady Highpole, but she's not totally on her own. She has a butler, a cook, and a gardener. I do her accounts at work. She's a lovely lady. Any luck finding out what made that noise?"

"No," said Amelia, poking around under a hedge with a stick.

"Perhaps it was a fox or a bird in the hedge," Sally said.

Amelia didn't think so. "Can we keep looking?"

"I'm sorry, love, but we are already running late. We need to get our fast legs on if we are going to make it to school on time! Let's have a look on the way home. You can remember where it is, right next to the broken gate."

 13

Amelia nodded and trotted after her mother as she walked briskly towards town.

2

An Amazing Find

"Haven't you finished yet?" Amelia's best friend, Lilly, leaned over and looked at her maths book.

"Hmm?" Amelia looked up. She had been doodling dogs in the margins of her work. One was cheekily licking a long division sum.

"You haven't even started the second set. That's not like you. Look, I've finished all mine for once." Lilly pointed at the board. "We have to do all those sums before we can go out to break!"

"Oh, I made a start but..." Amelia looked at the dog doodles. A dog was what she wanted more than anything. It had been her tenth birthday a few weeks ago and secretly she had hoped she might be getting a puppy. Her mum had said it wasn't possible at the moment, with no one at home to look after it during the day. She had to make do with her favourite stuffed toy dog.

"I won't take long." Amelia got stuck into the

 16

sums again. Like her mother, she had a good head for numbers. She saw them as little puzzles, and before long, she had worked her way through the second set from the board. They grabbed their bags and went out for mid-morning break.

"Does your family have plans for Christmas?" Amelia asked Lilly as they walked around the playground, huffing on their cold hands.

"Yeah, we are going to see my grandparents, so that means a really long drive, and I have to share a room with my brother!" Lilly screwed up her face as if she had eaten something horrible. "How about you?"

"We don't have anything planned, but Mum has the whole holiday off work, so at least I won't have to go round my aunt's house. I'm really looking forward to spending the time with Mum, you know, after what happened in the summer holidays." Sally had booked three weeks off work in the summer and they had made lots of plans for how they would spend the time together. At the last minute, Mr. Gunder had insisted Sally come into work, and Amelia had spent every day at her aunt's house instead.

"Well, I think you're lucky. I'd love two weeks at home with nothing much to do. Instead, I'll be dragged round all my relatives' houses and I'll have to be on my best behaviour all the time." Amelia laughed; it would be hard for Lilly to be on her best behaviour for a whole two weeks.

"Come over and see me when you get back. I'm sure our parents won't mind." Amelia said.

"That would be great, and I'll ask my mum if I can call you when I'm away, then I can tell you all about how bored I've been!"

"It's freezing. Come on, I'll race you to the tree at the bottom of the playing field."

19

"Last one there is a rotten egg!" Lilly called out, laughing as they both took off like rockets.

Three o'clock finally came, and with it, the end of term. Amelia gave Lilly a hug, and they exchanged Christmas cards before they left the playground. Lilly's mum picked her up in the car. She waved frantically out the window as they drove off. Amelia's mum was waiting by the small gate, hopping from foot to foot in the cold.

"I think the temperature has dropped since this morning!" Sally said, giving her a big hug as she walked out of the playground. "Come on, let's get moving."

Amelia had forgotten all about the strange noise she had heard that morning until she saw the broken gate in the hedgerow on the way home.

"Please, Mum, can we have another look in the field?" She thought her mother would say no as it was so cold, but after a reluctant look down the road towards their house, she nodded. Sally walked up one side of the hedgerow, and Amelia the other. Amelia stopped and listened carefully. She thought she heard a rustling sound. Crouching down, she used a stick to push back the prickly

 21

hawthorn branches at the base of the hedge. There, in amongst the leaves, was something brown and furry.

"Oh, Mum, look, it's a puppy!"

Sally came rushing over to see. "Look at the poor little thing. It's shivering. Here, if I hold the bramble out of the way, can you reach it without hurting yourself?"

"I'll try." Amelia reached her arm in carefully. The little puppy looked scared and cold, and it scooted its bum back further into the hedge. "I can't quite reach it." Amelia pushed her arm in as far as it would go, but the puppy kept backing away.

22

"Try talking to it. Maybe it will come closer if it's not so scared. I'll try to hold the branch up a little higher."

Amelia started gently talking to the puppy. Instead of reaching, she put her hand down on the ground and talked quietly and softly.

"Hello, little puppy. I know you're scared, but we just want to help you. You must be cold, and hungry too. We have some leftover chicken in our fridge at home, I bet you would like some of that." Amelia's voice seemed to soothe the puppy, and it edged closer to her hand.

"That's it, keep going. You're doing great," Sally encouraged.

 23

"Good little puppy, let's get you warm and fed. My name is Amelia and I want to take good care of you." At last, the puppy came right up to Amelia's hand. It nudged her fingers, gave her a sniff, and then settled its head on her hand. Amelia slid her other arm slowly around the back of the little dog. Carefully and slowly, Amelia brought the puppy out from the hedge until finally, she could hold the shivering pup in her arms. It was the same size as a little loaf of bread, with shining black eyes and damp, shaggy fur.

"We need to get that little one home and warmed up," Sally said. "But first, we should make sure there aren't any others here."

Amelia and Sally split up, taking one side of the field each, looking along the hedges. Amelia stopped and listened hard. There was a large overflow pipe coming through from the other field, its opening almost at the bottom of a shallow ditch. She was sure she had heard a noise coming from inside the pipe. Amelia carefully scooted down the side of the ditch while holding the puppy. The puppy started wiggling around so much she nearly dropped it. The bottom of the ditch was slippery, but she got her footing and looked into the pipe. She could only see a short way in before it became inky black. Amelia held her breath and waited, but there were no more noises

25

from inside the pipe. The puppy, however, started scrabbling and twisting in her arms. Sally came over and stood at the edge, peering down.

"Seen anything?"

"No, I thought I heard some noises from the pipe, but I can't see anything in there."

"Come on up, then." Sally held out her hand to Amelia to help her up the side of the ditch. "I think we should go home. That pup will need food, water, and warmth," Sally said, "and it's getting dark." Amelia nodded. She unzipped her jacket and put the shivering puppy inside next to her body to keep warm on the rest of the walk home.

 26

3

Puppy at Home

"I'll get some towels and a hot water bottle. Do you think you can find something for the puppy to eat?" Sally said when they got home. Amelia nodded. She had read so many books on looking after dogs that she knew exactly what kind of foods would be right.

Amelia put the little dog down on the kitchen floor, where it looked around, confused. She opened the fridge and found some cold chicken and some rice from yesterday's dinner. She broke the chicken up into small pieces and mixed it in with the rice.

"This little one needs warming up." Sally said. She bent down to pat the puppy and looked her over. "She's a little girl! Her fur is all wet, and she's still shivering a little. Why don't you towel her off, Amelia, and I'll add some hot water to that food to warm it up a little." Sally put the kettle on, and Amelia bent down with the warm, fluffy towels that her mother had brought. She picked the puppy up and began to dry its fur.

"We should give her a name." Amelia said. She gently dried the pup. She thought about how cold and wet the puppy had been, and what might have happened if they hadn't been walking past that morning. "I think we should call her Lucky."

"I agree, that is a wonderful name," said her mother, bending down to rub Lucky's small head.

"What kind of dog do you think she is?" Amelia asked, as she put the pup down on the floor. Sally put the bowl of food in front of Lucky and looked at her as she began to gulp the warm chicken and rice down. She was brown and fluffy, with a white patch on her

29

chest and white feet. She had floppy round ears, lovely big eyes, and expressive eyebrows.

"I'm not sure. I think she is a bit of a mix," Sally said, giving Lucky a pat as she ate.

"Can we keep her, Mum?" Amelia asked, holding her breath, waiting for the answer.

"Well, now…" Her mum took a deep breath and sighed it out. "I know we both love her already, but I can't just say yes. She might belong to someone. There could be a family out there going crazy with worry about this little one."

"What if there isn't. What if she's a stray, or abandoned, and nobody wants her. Can we keep her then?"

 30

"Even if she doesn't belong to someone, it's a really big decision to take on a dog. It's a commitment for twelve years or more, and it needs careful thinking about. We need to make sure we can do it right—not just for us, but for the dog too. I have to work and you are at school all day." Sally looked at Amelia's disappointed face. "I'm not saying no, but I can't say yes either. I'm sorry, Amelia. I know that's not what you wanted to hear."

Amelia looked sad, but then she looked into Lucky's eyes, and she instantly felt better. Maybe there was a family out there looking for her, but Amelia had the feeling that she was meant to find Lucky, and Lucky was meant to find her.

Lucky finished up every scrap of chicken and rice, licking the bowl so much it scraped across the floor. Amelia took her out into the back garden to see if she needed to go to the toilet after eating. When they got back in, they found that Sally had made up a spot on the couch for Lucky with a blanket and a hot water bottle wrapped in a towel.

"Here, why don't you two cuddle up together while I make some dinner for us? You both look tired."

32

Amelia and Lucky got cosy on the couch together, the blanket over both of them. Lucky huddled up to the hot water bottle and Amelia stroked her head. Soon, Sally came through with two plates of pizza. "I thought you would want something you could eat on the couch."

"Thanks, Mum," Amelia said, eating one handed, the other on Lucky's back. She didn't have to worry about Lucky trying to eat the pizza, as she was fast asleep.

"I've been thinking, tomorrow we should put up some missing posters in town to see if anyone is looking for Lucky."

33

Amelia didn't want to, but she knew that if Lucky did have an owner, they had to try to find them. "I'd be really sad if we lost a puppy, so I'll help you with them."

"Thank you, love. I know it's not easy for you."

"Can Lucky sleep in my room tonight? She's so little, I don't think she should be on her own."

Sally thought about it for a bit. She looked at the pair of them cuddled on the couch together.

"Yes, I think that's a good idea."

 34

Later that evening, Sally folded some blankets into a little nest on the floor beside Amelia's bed. She refilled the hot water bottle and put it inside a soft, fluffy cover. Lucky was already fast asleep, so Amelia placed her gently on the little bed and pulled a blanket over her. Then she put her pajamas on and hopped into her own bed. Sally came in to say goodnight and check they were both okay.

"Lucky is still fast asleep. She must have been exhausted. You look pretty tired too." Sally gave Amelia a kiss on the head and pulled the covers up.

"Good night you two. Sleep tight!" She turned the light out, but left the door open a

35

crack as she always did. Amelia could still see Lucky in the orange light coming from the hallway. She could hear the soft sleeping sounds and see the blanket moving gently up and down. Before she knew it, she was fast asleep herself.

4

Search for an Owner

The next morning, Amelia woke up bright and early. Lucky had jumped onto the foot of her bed in the night and was cuddled up next to her feet on top of the blanket.

"You're the best dog ever," she said softly, stroking her head. Lucky woke up, stretched, and then started jumping all over the bed, pulling at the blanket with her teeth.

"Let's get you outside for some fresh air!"
Amelia pulled her dressing gown over her
pajamas and went downstairs to grab her
wellies. Lucky jumped and nipped at her
dressing gown tie as she walked. The small
puppy was just as energetic in the garden,
running up and down, looking in hedges, and
rolling on the wet grass. The fresh air had
woken her up, but Amelia's tummy rumbled.
Luckily, when they came in, Sally was already
making breakfast for them both.

"Here is some more chicken and rice for
Lucky. We can get some proper puppy food in
town today. I made porridge for us."

"Thanks, Mum!" Amelia tucked in to her breakfast. She was so hungry. Once they had cleared breakfast away, Sally took a photo of Lucky, and together they designed some missing posters on the computer. Sally printed them out, and Amelia used her gold pen to draw some stars on the top to draw people's attention.

"What will we do with Lucky when we are out?" Amelia asked. Sally paused.

"I hadn't thought of that. We can't take her with us, as she doesn't have a collar or lead yet. We will have to pick those things up in town today. Let's make her up a bed in the kitchen.

We can wipe the floor in there in case there are any little accidents when we are out."

Amelia took Lucky out to the garden again for a good run before they went out, then they made up a bed in the kitchen. They left some food and water, and Sally put the radio on so the house wouldn't be quiet.

"We will be as quick as we can, but we have quite a lot to do in town today. Still, I think Lucky will be fine. She still seems really tired after her ordeal."

"Bye bye, Lucky. We'll be back as soon as we can!" Amelia stroked Lucky's head, then they headed out.

 40

Little Ridlington was small enough that you could walk anywhere you wanted, but big enough to have interesting shops and a weekly market. First, they visited the pet shop and asked if they could put up a poster about Lucky in the window.

"Of course. Put the poster by the door there with the others. I haven't heard of anyone missing a dog," the lady behind the counter said. "Usually we are the first place they come to put up missing posters—here and the vet, of course."

"Yes, the vet. I want to make an appointment to get her scanned for a microchip," Sally said. "Let's call in there next

41

and put up a poster. But first, we need some things!"

Amelia chose a small, red collar with a heart-shaped name tag you could write on and a matching lead. She also picked out a cosy bed with pictures of bones on it. Sally gathered food and water bowls, some puppy food, a brush, and some dog shampoo. "How about getting some toys for her?" Sally said. Amelia looked at the back wall of the pet shop. It was covered from floor to ceiling with soft toys, balls, ropes and Frisbees.

"Let's have this one," she said, reaching for a fluffy bone. It squeaked as she took it off the hook. "This one too," she said, picking up a yellow ball that looked like it would bounce.

"Perfect, I think that's everything for now." Sally said.

They made several stops on the way to the vet to put up posters, including one near the town's Christmas tree. It was nearly as tall as a house and covered in lights that were on all day and night. Amelia loved it. There was a notice board on the side of the town hall next to the tree. Amelia stood on her tiptoes to reach it.

"I can't wait for Christmas this year," she said as she pushed the first pin into the poster.

43

The board was hard, and it hurt her thumb pushing the pin all the way in.

"I'm looking forward to spending the time together. I know this summer was hard," Sally said, putting pins on the other side of the poster. Amelia nodded.

"Never mind, Mum, now we can spend the whole Christmas holiday together. It'll be better than summer, I know it!" She pushed the last pin into the bottom corner.

"Well done. Right, off to the vet's now," Sally said, giving her shoulder a squeeze as they walked off.

Amelia always thought that it smelled funny in the vets. Although they didn't have

 44

any pets, they were regular visitors because her mum was friends with Amy, one of the vet nurses. Amelia loved popping in to see Amy because she could make a fuss of the animals in the waiting room.

"What a sweet puppy!" Amy said, looking at the picture of Lucky. "What a nice name you have chosen, Amelia."

"It just seemed to fit her. Do you have any missing puppies in your book?" Amelia asked.

"I don't think so, but I'll double check anyway." Amy opened a green-backed book and flicked to the last page. "No, nothing at the moment. There is a missing cat called Patches, but no dogs of any kind. You can put

 45

the poster up in the waiting room if you like, and I can call you if we hear of anything."

"I'd like to make an appointment to have her checked over please," Sally said.

"That's a good idea. We can scan her for a microchip at the same time. Can you manage this afternoon?" Amy said, opening the appointments screen on the computer.

Amelia went to put the poster up while Sally sorted out a good time for the appointment. She stood on a chair and reached really high to stick the poster to the wall so that everyone would see it when they came in. When she got down from the chair, Sally put a hand on her shoulder.

46

"Well done, Amelia. Come on, we will put a few more posters up and then we had better get home. I don't want to leave Lucky any longer than we have to."

They had to walk past Sally's office to put up the last poster. Sally strode quickly past, looking fixedly ahead, but Amelia glanced in the window of the accountants. She saw Mr. Gunder staring at her mother as she walked past, looking more angry than ever.

47

5

Trouble at Work

On the way home, Amelia wanted to ask if they could stop and have another look in the field, but just as they were approaching the broken gate, Sally's mobile phone rang. Amelia could hear the shouty voice of Mr. Gunder on the other end, although she couldn't make out the words he said.

"I arranged for this time off work months ago," Sally was saying. Amelia got a sick feeling in her stomach. It was happening again! Every time her mother tried to take some time off work, Mr. Gunder found an excuse to bring her back in. It had been happening all year—not just in the summer, but at Easter too.

"I have completed the accounts for all the clients in my portfolio. I am ahead on everything." Sally's voice was starting to rise as she spoke on the phone. Amelia knew how hard her mum had been working, often late into the evening, so she could get everything done in time for Christmas.

 50

"I'm sorry, but my sister is out of the country this time, Mr. Gunder. There is no one who can take Amelia at all." Amelia could hear Mr. Gunder really shouting on the other end of the phone now.

"Absolutely not! I am not going to ask a child to spend two weeks sitting in silence in an office! It's totally inappropriate." Now her mother was shouting. Amelia was shocked. Her mother was usually so calm and patient with people, even Mr. Gunder. "Not to mention that I have other responsibilities right now, unless you suggest I bring a puppy in as well as Amelia."

"A PUPPY!" This time, Amelia could hear the words Mr. Gunder roared through the phone. Sally had to hold it away from her ear. As Mr. Gunder continued to shout out of the phone, Amelia saw the look on her mother's face change. Her brow creased, but then her mouth became firm as she seemed to come to a decision. When Gunder had finally shouted himself out, she put the phone back to her ear and began talking in a cool, clear voice.

"Then I quit, Mr. Gunder. I am formally obliged to give you four weeks notice. Luckily, however, I am owed a total of five weeks paid holiday, which I will be taking in full with immediate effect. You may keep the few

 52

personal items I have on my desk. I sincerely hope I never see you again." Sally pressed hang up on the phone and sagged visibly, as if someone had let all the air out of her.

Amelia stood with her mouth wide open in shock. Sally looked up, and when she saw Amelia's face, she pulled herself together.

"Don't worry. I wasn't going to let him cancel yet another holiday," she said, putting an arm around Amelia's shoulder. "That man has lost all touch with reality, expecting a little girl to spend all Christmas sitting in an office. It's not even as if there is anything urgent to be done. I think I have put up with too much

53

for too long in this job, and that was the final straw."

"But, Mum, what will you do for money?" Amelia asked, worried. Her mum frowned, then she forced a smile.

"Well, he has to pay me for the next five weeks, so I've got a bit of time to sort something out. Don't worry, poppet, we'll be okay." She ruffled Amelia's hair. "Better off than Gunder. He might actually have to do some work for once!" They strode off for home to see how Lucky had got on without them.

As they approached the front door, they could hear whining noises from inside.

"Oh, Mum, that's Lucky. She sounds sad!" Amelia said, her voice full of concern. Sally fumbled as she tried to get the keys out and in the lock as quickly as possible.

"Poor thing. We weren't gone for long, but she doesn't know what's going on yet. Quick, in you go." Sally held the door open and Amelia ran in and opened the kitchen door to see utter chaos.

Lucky had torn the pillow they put down for a bed into pieces, and fluff covered the floor. The blanket also had a large hole torn in it. There was a puddle of wee on the floor near the sink, a chair leg which had been chewed to bits, and the poor kitchen door had the paint scratched off on the bottom half. One of the cupboard doors was open and tins of tuna and soup lay scattered on the floor. Lucky sat in the middle of the mess with the saddest look on her face that Amelia had ever seen.

"Oh, Lucky," she cried as she scooped the small pup into her arms.

"Oh my goodness!" Sally exclaimed, appearing in the kitchen door behind Amelia. "Why don't you get Lucky outside for some fresh air while I clean up in here." Sally's face looked tired, her mouth tight. Amelia nodded and dashed outside, holding Lucky tightly.

 56

Amelia talked softly to Lucky as she took her out into the back garden. She expected the pup to run around like crazy after being stuck in the kitchen all morning, but the little dog didn't want to leave her side. Amelia sat down and sighed. She should have been happy to be outside playing with a dog - it was what she had always wanted - but she felt worried about her mums job and about Lucky.

"I can't believe you did that to the kitchen, Lucky. What if Mum doesn't want to keep you now?" Lucky seemed to sense her mood and nuzzled her hand. It was hard to stay gloomy looking into such a sweet pair of eyes. Amelia remembered the ball from the pet shop and

57

took it out of her pocket. She threw it just a short way, and Lucky cautiously walked over to it. She gently picked it up and looked at Amelia.

"Good girl! Bring it here," she said, patting her legs and encouraging the pup. Lucky brought it back right away, and Amelia threw it again, just a little bit further. By the time Sally came to call them in for lunch, Amelia was laughing and Lucky was bounding around all over the place with the ball in her mouth, dropping it, and quickly grabbing it again when Amelia tried to take it.

"Looks like you two are having fun! Come on in, warm up, and get something to eat.

58

Anyway, it's starting to rain," Sally called out from the back door.

"Come on, Lucky!" Amelia called to the pup as she ran to the door. Lucky soon caught her up and bolted in the door ahead of her. "Good girl." Amelia gave her a pat when she caught up. "You're the best dog ever."

Lucky sniffed cautiously at her lunch of puppy biscuits and wet food. Sally put a bit of chicken and rice in there too, and soon she was gulping it down. Sally put some sandwiches on the kitchen table with a bowl of fruit for their lunch.

59

"I'll need to repaint that door," Sally said, looking at the scratch marks and flaking paint, "and we'll need a new chair."

"Lucky didn't know she was doing anything wrong. Are you cross with her?" Amelia said anxiously.

"No, I'm not cross, not anymore." Sally sighed. "The poor thing was probably going crazy trying to find us. Never mind, we have a lead and collar now, so we don't have to leave her at home on her own anymore."

They sat chewing their sandwiches and looking at Lucky. The little dog had already finished her food and was having a big drink of water. She looked up, shook herself, and

 60

then came over and wiped her wet, furry face on Amelia's trouser leg. Amelia and Sally laughed. Lucky headed over to her new bed and lay down for a nap.

"Well, I'm glad you are both full. You have twenty minutes before we have to head out again. We have to take Lucky for her check over at the vet's. I've got to make a call to the animal shelter to see if anyone has reported her missing there."

 61

The nearest animal shelter was miles away, just outside the city. Amelia was feeling nervous about this. What if they found a microchip in Lucky and they had to return her to the owner? What if the shelter had heard of someone missing a puppy? Or offered to take her in? She already loved Lucky and would be heartbroken to lose her, but she knew the right thing was to check in case she was missing from a loving home. But if no one was missing her, how on earth had she ended up in a field all by herself?

6

Escape!

"Time to get your coat on, Amelia!" Sally called through. Amelia and Lucky came bundling out of the living room door.

"What did the shelter say?" Amelia asked nervously.

"They haven't had any enquiries about a missing puppy," Sally said. Amelia felt a wash of relief go through her. She sat down and started pulling her wellies on. It looked like rain outside and they had a long way to walk.

"I told them about Lucky. They said it's a good job we can look after her at the moment because they are full. The only other shelter in the county shut recently so they are overwhelmed. I'm not sure what we are going to do long term, as I need to find a new job quickly and I wouldn't want to leave her on her own all day." Sally sighed. "Well, lets get going to the vet's."

"Can I put the collar and lead on, Mum?" Amelia was hopping from foot to foot, looking eager. Sally smiled and nodded, holding the small red collar out to her. She

 64

carefully buckled it around Lucky's neck,
adjusting it to be just the right size. Lucky sat
down and scratched at her neck for a bit, the
name tag jingling, then she lay down on the
floor and tried to rub the collar off on the rug.

"You silly thing," Amelia laughed. "You'll
like it because now you can come out with
us!" She clipped the lead onto the collar and
Sally opened the front door.

"Keep a tight hold on her," Sally said. "We
don't want her to get lost again!" Amelia had a
good grip on the lead, but Lucky was so light
that even when she pulled it hardly felt like
anything.

 65

"She's trying to run everywhere at once!" Amelia said, as Lucky danced around on the end of the lead.

"We will do some proper lead training with her soon. I'll show you how," Sally said, "but let's just get today out of the way first. For the moment, if she pulls, just stop walking and be really boring. When she stops pulling, carry on walking like normal. It will stop bad habits forming."

Amelia did her best. At first, she thought it would take them forever to get into town, as she had to stop every few steps, but soon Lucky got the idea that she could get where she wanted to go if she didn't pull. Amelia

 66

looked up. The sky had darkened and the first spots of rain pattered onto her face. When they got to the broken gate, Lucky stopped and started whining.

"I think she wants to go in the field, Mum," Amelia said.

"I'm sorry, love, but we have to get going if we're going to get to the vet on time. We can take her in the field on the way back home if it's not too wet."

Amelia nodded and encouraged Lucky to come along. She sat down and wouldn't move, so Amelia picked her up and carried her for a short distance before she put her down again.

Finally, she started trotting nicely along on the lead again.

It had started to rain heavily by the time they arrived at the vets. Sally shook her umbrella and Amelia stamped her wet feet when they got inside. They took a seat near the window and saw the rain go from heavy to downpour outside.

"Let's hope that's lifted by the time we leave," Sally said. Amelia nodded, but really she was sitting with her stomach in knots, worrying about the scan they were about to have.

"Sally, Amelia, can you come through now?" Amy called from the corridor. Amelia's heart skipped a beat. She picked Lucky up and held her close as they went in.

"Can you put her on the table for me?" Caroline, the vet, said kindly when Amelia got into the consulting room. Amelia nodded and put a soggy Lucky onto the table. She immediately shook herself, sending water flying in all directions, then stood there with her fur all puffed out.

"Oh dear, now we're all wet!" Caroline said. "Let's have a look at you." Caroline gently felt Lucky's tummy, had a look at her eyes and her teeth. She got her stethoscope out and listened to her chest in several places.

69

"She seems a little thin, but otherwise very well. She is a very lucky puppy that you found her, especially as the nights get so cold and wet at the moment. Lets scan her for a microchip." Amelia held her breath as Caroline got the scanner out and ran it over Lucky's back.

"No, nothing," she said eventually. "It looks like Lucky is going to be with you for a bit longer, at least." Amelia sagged with relief.

"Is there anything we need to do?" Sally asked.

"You will need to feed her up a bit, make sure she gets lots of fresh air and exercise, but otherwise I'm very happy with her. Amy will

70

give you a wormer and some flea treatment on your way out. Any problems or worries, give us a call."

Sally thanked Caroline and went to the desk to pay. Amelia and Lucky stood at the doorway, looking at the rain.

"It's not going to lift," Sally said from behind them. "We might as well get going and get it over with, so we can be nice and warm at home."

They walked hunched over, with eyes screwed up against the rain on the way home. It was three in the afternoon, and the sun was already low in the sky; it would set soon. The rain lashed down at an angle, the wind

71

blowing so hard they had to lean into it at times. Amelia's hand was freezing cold holding the lead. Although she had gloves on, they had become soaked with the rain. When they got to the field with the broken gate, Lucky started pulling again. Suddenly, she jolted so hard on the lead that it pulled Amelia's soggy glove right off her numb hand. Amelia cried out as she saw the lead fall to the ground with the glove still attached. Lucky scooted under the gate and started running across the field.

"No!" Amelia shouted, and jumped over the gate after her.

7

Danger in the Field

Amelia ran her hardest across the field. Her feet slipped and slid in the mud, her wet wellies slapping against her legs. Sally was right behind her, not doing much better. Lucky was small and light and was able to dash across the ploughed field like a rocket, her feet hardly touching the ground. Amelia's breath burned in her chest as she tried to catch up, the rain stinging her eyes.

"No, Lucky, come back!" she shouted desperately. She slipped right over, her outstretched hands breaking her fall. Both her arms sank up to the elbows in the soft mud. She felt tears pricking her eyes as she watched Lucky getting further away as she tried to free herself from the sucking mud. Almost straight away, she felt her mother's arms around her chest, pulling her out of the swampy field and setting her back on her feet.

"Come on, love, we can catch her," Sally shouted over the wind, and they set off at a run again. They both slipped and slid across

 74

the boggy field, the icy rain making everything worse. It was starting to get dark now, making it difficult to see far over the field. Sally got her winter torch out of her bag and shone it ahead of them. The mud stuck to Amelia's boots, making them heavy and clumsy so that running became almost impossible.

At last, Lucky stopped running. As they got closer, they could see that her lead had caught firmly on a branch near the ditch with the concrete pipe. She was jumping up and down and barking at something they couldn't quite see.

"Look, Mum, down there!" Amelia called out. As they got closer, they could see that

 75

down inside the ditch there was an older dog, soaking wet and covered in mud. It was standing in the gushing water of the overflow pipe, desperately pulling and tugging at something inside.

"We need to get her out" Sally said. She checked Lucky's lead was secure before stepping carefully down into the ditch, using a branch to steady herself. Then, Sally reached up and held Amelia's hand as she helped her down the slippery slope. The water was just deep enough to go over the top of Amelia's welly boots, making her feet cold and wet.

"Here, hold the torch," Sally said, handing it over to Amelia. "I'll try to help the dog."

76

Amelia pointed the torch at the pipe so that Sally could see better. They could see the dog was trying with all its might to pull at a tangle of roots that were blocking the pipe entrance. It pulled and tugged, bracing its feet against the edge of the pipe as the water gushed around it.

"That wasn't there yesterday," Amelia said.

"It must have washed down the pipe with all the rain. Can you shine the torch right inside?" Amelia did as Sally asked and gasped.

"I can see a puppy!" Amelia shouted, pointing with her other hand. It was hard to see, but it was just the other side of the muddy roots in the pipe.

 77

"She must have had her litter inside," Sally called out over the noise of the rain and the gushing water. "All this rain has made it dangerous, and now she can't get her puppy out. Come on, lets try to pull it out."

Amelia put the torch in her pocket and gripped onto the roots with Sally, and they both heaved and pulled as hard as they could.

"It's no good, it's wedged," Sally said. The older dog had stopped tugging and was desperately circling their legs. They could hear the cries of the puppy behind the tangle.

"I'll keep pulling. See if you can find a strong stick," Sally said. Amelia looked around. It was really getting dark now. She shone the torch side to side as she walked up the ditch. Finally, she found a broken fence post.

"Here, Mum, is this any good?" she said, offering it to Sally, who was still pulling at the roots.

"That's great. I'll try to lever this bit free. Can you keep pulling on the roots?"

Amelia nodded. She gripped the smaller roots at the bottom and began pulling. Sally used the fence post as a lever to prize free the largest root wedged across the pipe entrance. Amelia could see the worry on her mother's face. The cries of the pup inside the pipe stopped and her heart went cold. She pulled harder than ever, and the muddy dog jumped up and pulled too.

Suddenly, the root ball started to move. Amelia pulled with all her weight, digging her wellies into the mud at the base of the pipe, and with a lurch, the whole lot came out at once. She landed on her backside, with the roots in her lap.

"Well done!" Sally cried, helping her back to her feet. "Let's help this puppy."

Amelia reached inside with her arm until she could feel something soft, warm, and soggy. She grabbed the puppy by the scruff of the neck and pulled it out. Amelia hardly dared look as she cradled the wet bundle in her arms. The mother dog jumped up to lick the puppy, and Sally put a hand on its little chest.

"I can feel it breathing," she said with relief. "Can you put it inside your jacket?" Amelia unzipped her coat and tucked the pup inside where it could be warm.

Sally shone the torch into the pipe again, but as she did so, the mother dog jumped up and into the pipe, disappearing further back behind some leaves. She came out again a moment later with another puppy in her mouth. The soaking wet dog offered the whimpering puppy to Sally, who took it with

81

surprise before the dog jumped back into the pipe again.

"There's one left," Sally said, peering into the pipe with the torch. "It's stuck in some more branches. I can't reach it, but the mother dog is trying to pull it out."

"Go on, you can do it!" Amelia called to the dog. Amelia's heart felt like it stopped beating as they both watched the dog pulling at the branches in the pipe. At last they came loose—just in time, as a large gush of water came down the pipe, sweeping both mother and puppy up with it.

"Yes! That's it!" Amelia cried out in joy as the mother dog found her feet and grabbed the wriggling puppy. Amelia finally took a breath. The mother dog came jumping out of the pipe with the last puppy in her mouth. They both crouched down, hugging the mother dog and each other. Tears of relief streamed down Amelia's face as she laughed and held all three wet puppies to her.

"Well done, girl, well done," said Sally, ruffling the wet fur on the mother dog's head.

It was fully dark now. Amelia could see the lights of the manor house in the distance and thought for a moment she could hear music. Sally shone the light of the torch around. Lucky was still barking and jumping up and

 83

down, her lead attached to the branch. Amelia scrambled up the bank and managed to undo it. Sally passed the puppies up to her and then climbed up the bank herself, the mother dog following.

"We need to get this lot home and in the warm and dry," she said. "Not to mention us. You're soaked through, Amelia!" Amelia looked down at herself. Her coat was covered in mud, her wellies were full of water, and her trousers were soaking. She was freezing cold, but she found she didn't mind at all. She was just so excited and relived to have rescued all the puppies.

"Can you manage Lucky and one other puppy?" Sally asked. Amelia nodded. She held firmly to Lucky's lead. She still had the other puppy tucked into her coat. Sally held one puppy under each arm.

"What about the mother?" Amelia asked.

"Don't worry, she will follow wherever her puppies go," Sally said.

Once they were back on the road, it was a short but cold trudge home. The mother dog stuck close to their sides, checking on the puppies all the time. The rain stopped just as they got to the gate.

"Typical," said Sally, closing the gate behind them. "It's been pouring for hours, but now

85

we're home, it's dry!" They both laughed, relieved to have brought the dogs safely home, and looking forward to warming up inside.

8

More to Love

"I don't know, yesterday morning we didn't have any dogs at all, and now we've got five!" Sally said as they looked at the bedraggled pups warming up in the bath. The poor dogs had been freezing and covered in mud. They had toweled them off when they got in, but they had still been shivering and dirty. The little dogs seemed happy enough now in the warm water, and their mother had jumped in to join them. She was now licking them each in turn, as if checking them over and over. The bath water was black with mud, but the dogs all seemed clean enough now.

"Three girls and two boys," Amelia said. "I already named Lucky, but I was thinking Honey for the other girl because of her fur."

"Sounds good, and how about the two boy puppies?"

"Well, this one has fur the colour of chestnuts, so I thought Conker," Amelia said, stroking the dark brown puppy, "and this one has white feet, so maybe Socks?"

 88

"That sounds perfect. It must have been quite an ordeal for them all, especially this one," Sally said, patting the mother dog on the head. "It's been really cold, and goodness knows how she has been feeding them. I think we should call the mum Meggy, like my grandmother. She was full of courage, and this girl here is the same."

"I was so scared when Lucky pulled the lead out of my hand, but I'm so glad she did because otherwise we would never have found them," Amelia said. She couldn't bear to think about what might have happened to the puppies if they hadn't been able to clear the roots from the pipe.

89

"Well, we did find them, and we will do our best for them, so let's not dwell on what might have been," Sally said.

"I've got all the towels ready now. Shall we start getting them out of the bath?" Amelia asked as she shook out the last of the big fluffy towels.

"Yes, lets get these little ones dry and in front of the fire. We can get them all fed, and then it's bath time for you too, young lady. You're not much better than they were!"

"And you, Mum!" Amelia laughed. It was true—she had mud in her hair, under her nails, everywhere, and so did Sally, who also had a big streak of mud across her forehead.

They had quickly changed out of their wet clothes when they got in, but they were still filthy. They had spent every moment since caring for the dogs.

They wrapped the pups in warm towels, and the mother dog jumped out of the bath and shook herself, soaking everyone before Amelia could throw a towel over her. Soon, all the dogs were all fed and resting in front of the living room fire, the smell of damp dog rising off them. Amelia was also clean from the bath and sat cosy and warm in her pajamas and fluffy dressing gown. Sally had gone up to have a bath. It felt so good to be clean and dry, have a full tummy, and to be surrounded by wonderful dogs. The crackling of the fire and the soft snoring of the dogs made Amelia feel sleepy. The next thing she knew, her mother was putting a pillow under her head and a blanket over her.

"Sweet dreams, darling," she said as she kissed her on the forehead, but Amelia was already fast asleep.

9

Preparing for Christmas

The next morning, Amelia woke early to the sound of yipping and barking. The puppies were playing a game of chase in the hallway, while Meggy lay curled up by the embers of the fire. Sally emerged from her bedroom, running her hands through her hair.

"Whatever time do they call this?" she said, making a beeline for the kettle. "It's going to be a two tea morning today, I think."

They only had one dog bowl, so Amelia got out a variety of soup bowls and plates to put dog food in for the four puppies and Meggy. Lucky seemed to be in charge of all the pups; when she came in to eat all the others followed. Amelia had to refill the water bowl three times. After they had eaten, Amelia took them all out into the garden. Sally had to clean up some overnight messes, but seemed to be in a good mood.

"Pancakes, Amelia, come on in and get them! You can let the dogs play outside if they are having a good time." The dogs didn't want to stay outside, but all came in buzzing around Amelia's feet.

"What are we going to do with five dogs?" Sally was saying, spreading jam on a fat pancake. "Perhaps I could have found someone to look after one dog while I went to work, but five…" She sighed and looked around. "And we don't exactly have room in the house for that many dogs."

Amelia felt worried. She already loved Lucky so much, and all the other dogs too now. She didn't want any of them to leave.

"But the shelter is full, so they have to stay with us, right, Mum?"

95

"Yes, they do for now." Sally sighed. "I've got to get my thinking cap on though. After all, I did quit my job yesterday."

Amelia frowned, but it was hard to stay glum for long. The puppies were wrestling and playing with each other, and Lucky started pulling on her trouser leg.

"You had better try to wear those puppies out with a ball game or something," Sally said, laughing. "We will have to pop out again. We have got a lot more stuff to buy from the pet shop today! It's the last day it's open before Christmas, after all."

Christmas! With all the excitement of the last few days, Amelia had almost forgotten.

They always put the Christmas tree up on the last day of school, but they had found Lucky on the way home and forgotten all about it. She hadn't finished making her mother's Christmas present yet either. Amelia had been making her a pen holder out of cardboard tubes. She was decorating it with pictures of things that Sally loved. She was carefully cutting them out and gluing them on. It was nearly finished. She had hoped it would cheer her mother up whenever she looked at it at work, but now her mother didn't have a job. Amelia's forehead crinkled.

"I know it's been a bit crazy the last few days, but we'll put the tree up tonight, and

97

tomorrow we will start our Christmas baking," Sally said. It was almost as if she had read Amelia's mind. "We might have to do things a little differently this year, but it certainly won't be a boring Christmas!"

Amelia smiled. She knew that this Christmas was going to be amazing, whatever happened.

At the pet shop, Sally gave the lady behind the counter a poster of all the dogs they now had at their house. She explained that instead of one missing puppy, they were now caring for five homeless dogs.

"I'll put this up, but we still haven't had anyone asking about it. I expect you will need some more food, then?"

"Yes," laughed Sally, "and quite a few other bits besides!" After leaving the pet shop with bulging bags, they made a quick stop at the vets. Amy and Caroline said that they would stop by after work that day to check the puppies and the mother over.

On the way home, Amelia looked over the field where they had found the dogs and saw the manor house in the distance. There seemed to be a party going on, with lots of cars outside, people arriving, and snatches of music wafting across the field.

"That's unusual," Sally said. "I don't think I have ever seen a party at the manor house in all the years we have been here, but recently I've noticed a few."

Amelia winced as they approached the front door, wondering what chaos they would find inside this time. Luckily, now the dog family was all together it looked like they had entertained each other rather than destroying the house.

After supper, Sally started bringing in box after box of Christmas decorations from the shed, including the long box that held the Christmas tree.

 100

"Each year I keep meaning to get a real tree, and each year we don't seem to get round to it, but old faithful will do us proud, I'm sure," Sally said.

"I don't mind, Mum," Amelia said as she got the tree out of the box. It came in three parts that you had to slot together, and then you had to spend ages fluffing up the branches. Sally put on some Christmas music, and they got to work. Normally, this was much easier and calmer, but this year they had a whole lot of extra help.

"Get off, Conker! No, Honey, leave that alone!" Amelia said, trying to fluff the branches, and keep the puppies off the tree

101

and out of the box of decorations all at the same time. Socks was running around with a bell in his mouth, making a tremendous racket. Meggy had made herself a nest out of the tinsel and looked like she had settled in for the night. In Amelia's imagination, putting up the Christmas tree with the puppies had been a lot more fun than this.

"Shall I shut them out?" Sally asked.

"No, I can manage," Amelia said. The only thing worse than trying to put the tree up with the puppies was putting the tree up without the puppies! She didn't know how long they would have them for and wanted to make the most of every minute, even if those minutes were full of frustration!

Amelia and Sally stood back to look at their hard work. They had to make some changes to the way they normally decorated the tree, as the puppies wanted to eat or destroy any bauble they could get their paws on. The tree was crammed with tinsel, lights and decorations from the middle up, leaving the bottom half completely bare! Sally had moved boxes and tables so that the puppies couldn't reach any of the wires from the lights that ran down the back of the tree to the plug sockets.

"I think it's lovely, Mum," Amelia said, admiring the tree.

"I think it will be a Christmas to remember!" said Sally.

Not long after they had finished, there was a knock on the door. Sally showed Amy and Caroline into the living room, where they both had a good laugh at the Christmas tree. Caroline checked over all the puppies and Meggy too.

"They all seem to be a little skinny, but fine otherwise. Nothing that some good food won't fix. I brought my scanner to check for microchips just in case."

Amelia's stomach flipped over. She had forgotten about that. What if Caroline found an owner? But of course someone must own Meggy. She was far too well behaved and friendly to be a wild dog.

Caroline ran the scanner over all the puppies, and over Meggy last, but found no microchips. Amelia was secretly relieved.

"What will you do with them all?" Amy asked.

"I honestly don't know," Sally answered, "but they'll be here for Christmas, at least. I'll have to make a decision in the new year though." Amelia's heart leapt. They might not be able to keep the dogs forever, but at least she could enjoy a special Christmas with them.

10

A Knock on the Door

Christmas Eve came at last. Everyone seemed excited, including the puppies. They were running around, nipping and pulling at Amelia's socks and trouser legs as she walked from the kitchen into the living room. She had to slide her feet across the floor without lifting them up so she didn't stand on any puppies on her way through.

"It's no good - we need to take this lot out for a walk," Sally said, putting down the job vacancies paper to watch the shuffling procession of child and dogs.

"Good idea, Mum. I'll get my coat on."

After a lot of running around, they finally managed to get leads on all the dogs. Meggy seemed to know what was going to happen and was sitting patiently at the door, but the puppies were still running all over the place.

"I'll take Meggy, Conker, and Socks if you can manage Lucky and Honey," Sally said. Amelia grabbed the leads of the two excited puppies and soon they were ready to go. Walking the puppies was hard work. Although they were small and light, they kept trying to go in different directions and Amelia had to untangle their leads every few minutes. Sally wasn't doing much better. Meggy walked nicely on one side, but Conker and Socks seemed to do their best to trip her up on the other side.

"I hope this wears them out!" Amelia said, smiling as Honey barked at a gatepost.

"It's certainly wearing me out!" Sally replied.

When they got back, Amelia spent some time finishing up the present she had been making for her mother. She had cut out some pictures of the dogs from a spare lost poster and stuck them onto the pen holder, so they could always remember them. She let the glue dry and then carefully wrapped it up. Just as she had finished she heard the phone ring. Then, a moment later, her mother called up the stairs.

"Amelia, it's Lilly on the phone."

"Please, please tell me you have some interesting news," Lilly said, speaking so quickly Amelia couldn't get a word in edgeways. "I've been crazy bored since we got to my nan's house. All everyone wants to do is sit around talking or watching really rubbish telly. I've already been in trouble twice—once because I accidentally ate all the jam tarts, and then because I let slip about my brother's Christmas present. He doesn't mind. He's chuffed to bits he's getting a bike. So tell me what you've been doing," she said, finally pausing. Now it was Amelia's turn to speak, she found she couldn't stop talking either. Lilly squeaked with delight when she told her about finding the puppy in the field, and squeaked even louder when she told her about finding the rest of the family. She let out a sigh when she told her about Sally quitting her job.

"So, what are you going to do with five dogs? Are you going to keep them all? You have to keep them at least until I get back

111

from my nan's and I can meet them. I can't believe all this is happening when I'm away!" Lilly said.

"They should still be here when you get back. The shelter doesn't have room for them. I don't know what we will do. I don't want any of them to leave, but Mum says we don't have room for five dogs in the house, and she needs to find a new job. I'm really worried that someone will claim them, or we will have to give them away."

Lilly cheered her up by telling her funny stories about their Christmas trip away. When she got off the phone, she felt much better.

That evening, when it got dark, Amelia hung her Christmas stocking up in the living room. Sally made hot chocolate with marshmallows and Amelia snuggled down with some of her favourite Christmas books. The dogs were dozing in front of the fire, sleepy and well behaved for once. Lucky was sleeping with her head on Amelia's foot. Sally was in the kitchen humming while she prepared the turkey for Christmas lunch. The peace was broken by the sound of the doorbell ringing.

"Amelia, can you quickly grab that? I've got turkey on my hands. I need to wash them," Sally called through.

113

"Sure, Mum," Amelia said as she jumped up to go to the door. Sensing the excitement, the dogs started to stir too.

When Amelia opened the door, she saw a sturdy old lady with curly grey hair standing there in a thick, warm coat. A tall man in a smart black coat stood behind her, and a very smart old fashioned looking car was parked on the road outside their house.

"Hello, dear, is your mother at home?" the old lady started, but then stopped, staring behind Amelia. Suddenly, she dropped to her knees and held her arms out. Meggy came bursting between Amelia's legs, tail wagging

 114

furiously as the old lady hugged and patted her.

"Good girl, Toffee, oh, what a good girl!" she said, her eyes brimming with tears. "I thought I had lost you forever!"

11

Lady Highpole

Amelia stood open-mouthed in the doorway until she felt a comforting hand on her shoulder as her mother came to stand behind her.

"Hello, I'm Sally. Please come in, Lady Highpole," Sally said. Amelia looked wide-eyed at her mother, and then at the lady crouching down, hugging Meggy. Could she really be Lady Highpole from the manor house?

"Thank you," the lady said, standing up and wiping her eyes with a small white handkerchief. "I know you, don't I? From the accountant's office?"

"Yes, I work for Mr Gunder—or, I used to. Come on in and get warm." Sally and Amelia stood back, allowing Lady Highpole into the hallway.

"This is Walter," Lady Highpole said as the tall, well-dressed man came in through the door behind her. Amelia looked questioningly at her mother, but Lady Highpole smiled, leaned closer to her and lowered her voice.

 118

"He will tell you he is the family butler, and that is his job, but really he is a very dear friend." Walter went slightly pink and looked awkward.

Lady Highpole was just taking her gloves off when they heard an almighty crash from the kitchen. Sally and Amelia ran in to see that Socks and Conker had pulled the turkey onto the floor. Stuffing had splattered everywhere, and both dogs were ripping enthusiastically at the top of the bird.

"Oh no! Off you get," Sally said, picking up the mess of a turkey and putting it on the side. "I don't think that's edible anymore," she added as she looked at the smashed bird with bite marks taken out of it.

"Oh dear!" Lady Highpole said as she looked through the kitchen door. Just as she spoke, there was another crash from the living room.

"What now?" Sally cried, washing the turkey off her hands again as Amelia sped into the living room to see what had happened. The half-decorated Christmas tree had been pulled over and lay bent at an odd angle over the coffee table. Presents under the tree had been crushed where it had fallen. Lucky and Honey were playing tug of war with a length of tinsel hanging off one end of the tree. Amelia wrestled the tinsel from the dogs and pushed the tree back up as best she could. It now stood with its decorated top half at a crooked angle. Sally came in drying her hands, followed by Lady Highpole and Walter.

"Oh dear, it looks like old faithful has had it," Sally said.

"I'm terribly sorry. I think this is all my fault," Lady Highpole said. "I should have called to let you know I was coming, but

 121

when I saw Toffee on your poster in town, well, I just had to come here right away."

"I had no idea that Meggy—sorry, Toffee—was your dog," Sally said. "We would have taken her straight up to the manor house if we had known. Please, have a seat, Lady Highpole. I think we could all do with a cup of tea."

"You can call me Figgy, dear," said Lady Highpole. "A cup of tea would be lovely. We have a lot to talk about." Figgy Highpole sat down, but Walter stood by the window near the door.

Amelia tried to tidy up quickly while Sally made tea. Meggy—or as Amelia now knew she was called, Toffee—didn't leave Figgy's side. She sat with her head resting on the old lady's lap while getting a head scratch. Amelia scrambled about on the floor, trying to pick up baubles and decorations that had fallen off the tree in the crash. She was glad to be doing something, as it allowed her to hide the tears that were threatening to spill down her cheeks.

"Please, don't worry on my account," said Figgy Highpole. "I've had dogs my whole life. I know the mischief they can cause! Come and sit down." She patted the couch next to her and Amelia reluctantly padded over to sit down, trying to form a smile. Figgy looked sympathetic. She leaned in and lowered her voice as if sharing a secret. "My father once had a Great Dane called Thomas who ate a whole Victoria sponge at one of his summer parties. It didn't stay down for long though— he was sick in my Aunt Grey's handbag!" She sat back and laughed at the memory. "Gosh, she was furious! My father had to pretend to be very cross with Thomas, of course, but really he didn't like Aunt Grey very much, and I saw him giving Thomas a slice of roast beef later that day! Why don't you tell me all about what's been happening. Are these Toffee's puppies? Because she wasn't expecting any when I last saw her!"

 124

Sally brought in tea on a tray and smiled to see the two getting on so well. She let Amelia explain in excited tones about how they had found the puppy, and put the posters up, and how they had found Toffee and the other puppies in the field. It was quite a story, and Figgy sat forward, her tea quite forgotten, as she listened intently. She even wiped away a tear when Amelia described the puppies in the storm drain and Toffee's desperate efforts to rescue them.

"Gosh," Figgy said, sitting back, when Amelia had finally finished. "Well, now, I bet you are wondering how my lovely dog Toffee

125

ended up having puppies in a field all by herself!" Amelia and Sally both nodded.

"I'll start at the beginning. You see, for some time now I have been wanting to open an animal sanctuary up at the manor house. I've always been soft when it comes to animals, ever since I was a girl. I have so much time on my hands since my husband's passing, and I really wanted a new focus in life. So I decided to visit my good friend, Biddy, who runs an animal sanctuary at Hanford Hall. I have been there four months! She has shown me so much, and now I feel quite confident to open my own sanctuary. Anyway, Walter came with me to Biddy's, and I left Toffee at home

 126

with my nephew, Mark, who promised to look after the manor and Toffee while I was away. Well, it seems he was utterly useless at both! He had one party after another, with people staying constantly. During one of these events, a guest left the door open and poor Toffee escaped the house. This was just a few days after I left. My nephew thought Toffee would come home by herself. When she didn't, he gave her up for dead, but didn't have the courage to tell me!" Figgy shook her head, and Walter looked disgusted.

"I threw Mark out and told him never to darken my door again. I thought Toffee was gone forever. But when I saw your poster, I

127

asked Walter to drive me straight over here, and, well, what a surprise. Not just Toffee, but puppies too! I always planned to let her have just one litter, but not like this." Figgy ruffled Toffee's ears, and Toffee leaned her head against her knee. Sally smiled, but Amelia looked down at her hands. Lucky nuzzled her arm, but it didn't help the sad feeling go away this time.

"I'm really going to miss them," Amelia said. She was trying hard not to get upset, but her voice still wobbled. She could see how nice Figgy was, and how much Toffee loved her, but she was going to miss the dogs terribly—especially Lucky. They were

 128

supposed to at least have Christmas Day together. Amelia felt her lip tremble as she looked at Lucky.

"This must be very hard on you," Figgy said kindly. She looked around at the broken Christmas tree and the squashed presents and seemed to make a decision.

"Although this is going to be a wonderful Christmas for me, because I have my darling Toffee back, I can see it will be very difficult for you. You clearly love the dogs very much. Not to mention your poor Christmas tree, and your turkey doesn't seem to be edible any more. Why don't you both come and spend Christmas Day with me?"

"Oh, we couldn't put you to the trouble," Sally said, but Figgy waved her objection away.

"You two have given me a gift beyond price, not to mention that I do get a little lonely this time of year. Especially now I have given Mark the boot. My Christmas tree is not bent, we have an enormous turkey capable of feeding us all three times over, and Amelia can spend Christmas Day with the dogs. I think she will enjoy exploring the manor house and gardens. What do you say, Sally? Will you come? Really, you would be doing me a favour!"

"Oh, please, Mum, can we go? I really want to be with Lucky on Christmas Day, please!"

"Well, when you both put it like that, how can I refuse!" Sally said, her hands spread out in defeat. "We would be delighted to spend Christmas Day with you, Figgy."

"Perfect. Well then, Walter, will get this lot bundled up into the car, and I expect to see you both when you are ready tomorrow morning!"

12

Christmas at Last

Amelia woke up early on Christmas morning, but it didn't feel as special as it usually did. She came downstairs and saw her stocking full of presents, but all she could think about was how quiet the house was. She had become used to the noise and chaos of all the dogs, but most of all she missed Lucky. Amelia loved all the dogs, of course, but

Lucky had been something really special. She really had thought they would be able to keep her. There had been a special feeling straight away that they were meant to be together. Amelia took her stocking down from the fireplace and sat on the couch, looking at the bent Christmas tree in the corner of the room. Sally popped her head around the door.

"Good morning, sweetheart, and happy Christmas! I thought I heard you come down the stairs. I made us cinnamon waffles for breakfast. Do you want to open your stocking first?" Sally said, stepping into the room.

"I can smell the waffles. Can I have those first?" Amelia said quietly.

 134

Sally looked worried. "That's not like you. Normally you're desperate to see what Santa has brought you. Are you missing the dogs?" Sally said. Amelia nodded and started fiddling with the bow on her stocking.

Sally sighed. "Me too. They were a lot of work, but the house is really quiet without them!" Sally said. She sat by Amelia and gave her a big hug. "Don't worry, we will see them all today when we go up to the manor. Let's have breakfast, and then we can open our presents. After that, you can get dressed and we will go to the manor house early, okay?" Sally gave Amelia's arm a squeeze and Amelia

135

nodded, smiling for the first time that morning.

Amelia ate her waffles quickly. She felt a little better and enjoyed opening the presents in her Santa sock. Then they gave each other their special Christmas gifts.

"I absolutely love it!" Sally said when she opened the pen holder. "I will need to get organised if I'm going to find a new job, and this will be just the thing. Thank you, darling. I can see you put a lot of work into it. Now, here is your present from me."

Amelia tore the wrapping paper off to find a pair of trainers with wheels in the bottom.

"Wow, I've wanted these for ages! Thanks, Mum."

"You are very welcome. Now why don't you get dressed and we'll head up to the manor."

Amelia ran upstairs, brushed her teeth, and started getting dressed. As she was pulling some trousers out of the drawer, she heard the phone ring. Her mother answered it and began talking in hushed tones, taking the phone into the living room and shutting the door. It was probably her aunt again. She had been calling a lot over the last week. Amelia soon forgot all about it as she pulled her trousers on and hopped around on one leg,

137

trying to put a sock on her foot without sitting down.

"I'm ready!" Amelia called as she bounded down the stairs.

"Well, shoes on then. I'll get the coats," Sally said, putting the phone back on its cradle in the hallway.

The manor house made quite an impression on Amelia as they crunched up the gravel drive. It was so much bigger than she expected close up, with hedges cut into fancy shapes, neat lawns, and a fountain. There was a stone staircase leading up to a curved wooden door, with statues of two proud-

 138

looking dogs on either side. The air was cold
and sharp, but it was dry so they could wrap
up against the cold, and there was a lovely
fresh smell. Amelia was clutching a Christmas
card she had made the night before for Figgy.

As soon as the doorbell rang, they could
hear the barking of dogs from the other side of
the door.

"Quiet down, you lot," they could hear
Walter saying behind the door. There was a
scuffling, shuffling noise before the door
clunked and opened just a crack.

"Ah, hello, I do apologise, but the dogs all
seem to be trying to get out at once. Would
you mind squeezing in quickly?" Walter held

139

the door open just a little bit with his leg guarding the opening at the bottom. Amelia could see a lot of brown fur dashing around behind his leg.

"Of course!" said Sally. Amelia slipped into the door first, quickly followed by her mum. Walter didn't need to worry about the dogs escaping after that because they had all bundled on top of Amelia! She knelt down to see them and was quickly overwhelmed by licks and nuzzles as the puppies jumped up on her. She laughed and Sally laughed too, patting Toffee on the head.

"Wonderful, you came!" Figgy said as she came beaming out of one of the side rooms.

140

"They are very pleased to see you," she said, looking at the brown furry chaos on the floor. "Don't stand there in your cold things, come and get warm by the fire."

They walked into a large, warm room with a huge fireplace and an enormous Christmas tree at one end.

"It's a real one, Mum. I can smell it," Amelia said, breathing in the piney scent of the tree. There was a side table with small cakes, biscuits, and chocolates on it, and some chairs set out between the fire and the Christmas tree where Sally and Figgy sat. Amelia sat on the floor with the puppies,

141

happily munching a biscuit and trying not to let the puppies get it.

There were a lot of paintings of dogs and horses on the wall, and a photograph on a side table of a young lady surrounded by dogs.

"That's me, before I was married," Figgy said. "We have always had dogs. See that painting up there? That's a picture of my father with Thomas, the Great Dane I was telling you about yesterday." Amelia looked up at a large painting of a tall man standing with a proud and noble-looking grey dog.

"You would never guess that he's been sick in someone's handbag!" Amelia said. Figgy laughed and began telling many more stories

 142

about dogs behaving badly in the manor house.

Figgy's smile and hearty sense of humour was catching. Amelia and Sally found themselves laughing and telling stories themselves.

"I can't remember the last time I had this much fun," Figgy said eventually.

"I nearly forgot, I made you this," Amelia said, pulling a now rather crumpled card out from her trouser pocket.

"Why, thank you very much," said Figgy, opening it. "I will put it here in pride of place. I really hope you two will come and visit me more often now that we know each other. It

143

can be very quiet here these days. What I really like is a busy, noisy house. Mind you, it's a lot busier and noisier now that there are so many puppies running about the place! Which reminds me, I have something for you, Amelia." Figgy got up and rummaged around under the tree. She picked up a small present wrapped in red and gold paper and tied with a real ribbon. She handed it to Amelia, who looked at it curiously. When she opened it, there was Lucky's red lead and collar inside.

"Thank you, but I don't understand..." she said, holding it up.

"Well, it's a bit difficult to wrap up a puppy." Figgy laughed. "They keep wriggling when you try to put the paper on!"

"A puppy?" Amelia said.

"Yes, dear, I called your mother this morning to ask if I could give you Lucky to keep as your own. I could see quite clearly how much you loved her, and how hard it was for you to say goodbye last night. It seems to me that Lucky loves you too! She never leaves your side. So, what do you say, will you take her and look after her very well for me?"

"Yes! Yes, of course!" Amelia said. Her heart was swelling so big with the happiness of it all that she thought it might burst out of her chest. Lucky seemed to sense something good was happening too. She jumped up onto Amelia's lap and started licking her cheek.

"Is it true, Mum, is Lucky is mine to keep?" Amelia asked, almost breathless. Sally nodded, smiling hugely, and Amelia hugged Lucky close, tears coming to her eyes.

"That's so wonderful. Thank you so much! This is the best Christmas ever!"

"Well now, that's not all of my surprises. Sally, I know that you left that old miserly Gunder, and I don't blame you. He is such a rude man. The thing is that if I am going to be setting up my own animal shelter, I will need quite a bit of help with the paperwork

 146

and the financial side of things. Honestly, I'm not very good at paperwork; it's the animals that I love. I am wondering, would you come and work for me? It's so hard to find someone trustworthy these days. But seeing how you acted when you found my Toffee and her puppies, well, I think it just goes to show what good and honest people you both are."

"I, well…" Sally stuttered. "I'd be absolutely delighted to help you with your animal shelter. That would be wonderful. Thank you so much, Figgy!"

"I am delighted and relieved! You wouldn't believe the amount of time my friend Biddy

147

has to spend at a desk. Well, I think it's time to go through for lunch now."

The dining room was enormous and a wonderful feast had been laid out for them. A lovely big turkey was in the centre of the table, with lots of Yorkshire puddings, sausages, stuffing, and so many other little side dishes Amelia didn't know where to start. They ate until they could hardly move. They wore gold party hats, told terrible jokes, and Amelia noticed Figgy sneaking little bits of turkey to the dogs under the table.

When it was time to leave, Figgy clipped the red collar round Lucky's neck and handed Amelia the lead.

"I know you will take the very best care of her. Now you make sure to come and see me, Toffee, and the other puppies all the time. We will be waiting for you!"

"I will do, Figgy. I'll come all the time. Thank you so much again."

"No, thank you! You gave me my Toffee back safe and well. More than that, I think we will be very good friends. Come and see me any time!" Figgy said, and opened the door for them. Lucky looked up at Amelia and started pulling her towards the door, eager to get going.

"Goodbye. I'll come and see you tomorrow!" Amelia promised on her way out.

 149

Figgy stood waving at the doorway as Amelia and Sally walked down the drive. Flakes of snow began to fall gently from the sky. Lucky began to run round and round in circles at the end of the lead, trying to catch the snowflakes from the air with her mouth. Amelia and Sally looked at each other and smiled. This really had been the best Christmas ever!

Made in the USA
Las Vegas, NV
19 December 2024

14742902R00090